unit study guide for

G. A. HENTY'S

BY PIKE AND DYKE

A ◆ TALE ◆ OF ◆ THE ◆ RISE ◆ OF ◆ THE ◆ DUTCH ◆ REPUBLIC

BY

RICHARD G. MEDLIN

PrestonSpeed Publications
Pennsylvania

A note about the name PrestonSpeed Publications:
The name PrestonSpeed Publications was chosen in loving memory of our fathers, Preston Louis Schmitt and Lester Herbert Maynard (nicknamed "Speed" for his prowess in baseball).

**Unit Study Guide for G. A. Henty's By Pike and Dyke:
A Tale of the Rise of the Dutch Republic**
Copyright © 2001 by Richard G. Medlin

ISBN 1-887159-59-2

Published by
PrestonSpeed Publications
51 Ridge Road
Mill Hall, PA 17751
(570) 726-7844

TABLE OF CONTENTS

What is the purpose of the Henty study guides?

G. A. Henty's books offer readers accurate history, fascinating geography, refined language, admirable characters, and of course, great stories. The purpose of PrestonSpeed's Henty study guides is simply to help children learn as much from these wonderful books as possible.

What is included in these study guides?

As children read each chapter of the book, they answer **Chapter Questions** designed to help them follow the main events of the story and understand why these events occur. **Think It Over Questions** focus on moral and spiritual issues that come up in the chapter, and offer children an opportunity to think critically about such issues and to discuss them with their parents or teachers. Each lesson has an exercise designed to help children learn **Vocabulary Words** taken from the chapter, and **Activities**, such as map work, suggestions for research on topics related to the story, and "Just for Fun" projects.

These study guides also contain game-like **Reviews** of vocabulary words, **Articles** on special topics related to the book, and a major **Writing Assignment**. A list of the vocabulary words, solutions to vocabulary reviews, and maps are also included.

How are these study guides designed to be used?

PrestonSpeed's Henty study guides are intended to be used in homeschools or classrooms with children of middle-school ages or older. They are designed to be flexible, and can be used successfully in a variety of ways.

One approach is to have children complete one lesson each day. At that pace, an entire study guide takes between four and five weeks to finish. The time required to complete a lesson–including the assigned reading–is usually between one and two hours, but it will vary. (Some of the **Activities**, for example, can take quite a long time.)

Another, less intensive approach is to let children read two chapters of the book each day. Rather than answering the **Chapter Questions**, they can simply recite to you the main events of each chapter, discuss some of the **Think It**

Over questions, and do as many or as few of the **Vocabulary** exercises and **Activities** as you like. With this approach, the book can be finished in two to three weeks.

How do you spell . . . ?

Modern spelling of geographical locations sometimes differs from that which Henty used. Henty's spelling is used throughout these study guides, with modern spelling in parentheses when necessary.

About page references:

The page numbers referenced in these study guides correspond to page numbers in the PrestonSpeed editions of Henty's books. The number before the slash refers to the hardback and trade paperback editions; the number after the slash refers to the featherweight edition.

About the *By Pike and Dyke* study guide:

By Pike and Dyke tells the story of William I, called William the Silent, and his fight to free the Netherlands from Spanish rule during the years 1572-1584.

To use this study guide, the only resources you need are *By Pike and Dyke*, a dictionary, and either access to the internet or a good encyclopedia and a book of Rembrandt's paintings, which you should be able to find in a public library. If you would like to include related reading, younger students may like *Hans Brinker or The Silver Skates: A Story of Life in Holland* by Mary Dodge, or *The Wheel on the School* by Meindert de Jong. Older students may enjoy Alexandre Dumas' *The Black Tulip*, a novel set in the time of Johann de Witt, who governed the Netherlands from 1653-1672.

Be forewarned that *By Pike and Dyke* is the story of a way, and includes restrained descriptions of violence and cruelty. Also, please review two of the in-depth articles in this stude guide before you use them: **The Netherlands Today** discusses euthanasia and **Art of the Dutch Golden Age** reports a dishonorable episode in Rembrandt's life.

Read the Introduction

☐ When and where did Henty live?

☐ Why did Henty first start writing books?

☐ Is everything in this book true?

☐ What kinds of things would you expect to be true in this book?

Read the Preface

☐ Henty mentions three ways in which the struggle he writes about in *By Pike and Dyke* is unique. What are those three ways?

☐ What two things do Holland and Zeeland win as a result of this struggle?

☐ Against whom do they struggle?

☐ What transforms the ordinary people of Holland and Zeeland into heroes?

☐ What is their "one ally" before England joins the fight?

Think It Over

War is a terrible thing, yet the history of mankind is a litany of wars. Is war always wrong, or can there be such a thing as a "just war"? If so, under what conditions would war be justified? From what you have read in the Preface, do you think the Dutch war for independence was a just war?

Vocabulary

The following words are taken from the Preface. Find each word and, using the context as your cue, write down what you think it means. Now look up the words in the dictionary to see if you are right, and if not, correct your definition.

bigot
sublime
imbued
beleaguered
canon

Activities

- Find out more about Mr. Henty. Start with his publisher's home page on the internet, located at *www.prestonspeed.com*.

Read Chapter I

☐ What is happening in the Low Countries that disturbs Captain Martin and his friends?

☐ What does Captain Martin conclude that the people of England should do? Why?

☐ What acts of some of the people of the Low Countries especially anger Philip of Spain?

☐ Who are the Sea Beggars? What is their purpose? Why are they so desperate?

☐ Who is the Duke of Alva? What kind of man is he? How do you know?

☐ Who is De la Marck? What kind of man is he? How do you know?

Think It Over

In this chapter the sea captains argue about whether England should help the Dutch fight for independence from Spain. List the points they make both for and against England's involvement (see pages 4-7/4-8). Analyze them. Are any illogical? Immoral? Impractical? Which side do you think wins the argument?

Vocabulary

The definitions of the nouns below are provided for you. Write one paragraph (or if you really like a challenge, one sentence) that uses all five words correctly and still makes sense.

facsimile – copy, reproduction	page 2/2
rendezvous – meeting, get-together	page 3/3
mercenaries – hired soldiers	page 4/5
heretic – one who holds beliefs contrary to established religious doctrines	page 5/5
assent – agreement, approval	page 5/6

Activities

- "Mary's time" is mentioned on page 5/5. Who is Mary and what happened in England during her time?

- Find Rotherhithe (on the Thames River near London) on a map of England.

- Find a modern map of the **Netherlands**. Where is the Netherlands? What sea lies to the west? What country borders it on the south? On the east? Locate the following places on your map:

  Provinces – Friesland, North and South Holland, Zeeland, North Brabant
  Cities – Amsterdam, Rotterdam, Haarlem, Enkhuizen, Leiden, Maastricht
  Rivers – Rhine, Waal , Maas, Lek

- On a modern map of **Belgium** find the Schelde River and the cities of Ghent, Brussels, and Antwerp.

Read Chapter II

- [ ] How do the Sea Beggars use their one ally, the sea, to defeat the Spanish at Brill?

- [ ] What happens at Rotterdam? At Flushing?

- [ ] What is the significance of the meeting at Dort?

- [ ] What problems does the Prince of Orange experience as he comes to the Netherlands with his army?

- [ ] What happens on St. Bartholomew's Eve, and how does this affect the rebellion in the Netherlands?

- [ ] What is the "terrible news" that Captain Martin hears when he tries to find his relatives in Amsterdam?

- [ ] What does the letter for Captain Martin say?

Think It Over

Captain Martin is threatened with arrest because he "cursed and abused his Majesty the King of Spain, the Duke of Alva, the Spaniards, and the Catholic religion" (see page 35/35). In the United States, the Bill of Rights (the first ten amendments to the Constitution) gives us freedom of speech: "Congress shall make no law...abridging the freedom of speech or of the press." What are the advantages and disadvantages of freedom of speech? Are there any ways in which freedom of speech is limited today? Are there any ways in which freedom of speech is abused today? Does having "freedom of speech" mean you can curse someone, as Captain Martin did?

Vocabulary

Find these adjectives in Chapter II. First find the noun or pronoun that each adjective modifies, and then, using the context as your cue, match each adjective to its definition.

ribald	page 23/23
somber	page 23/23
clement	page 23/23
maritime	page 25/25
sanguine	page 25/26

dark and gloomy
merciful; compassionate
bordering the sea
funny in a coarse or vulgar way
hopeful; confident; cheerful

Activities

- Find out more about the Huguenots and the St. Bartholomew's Day massacre.

- Find the following places (indicated in **bold**) on the map on page 66 of this study guide: When **Brill (Brielle)** is taken by the Sea Beggars, Count Bossu brings Spanish troops from **Utrecht** to recapture the city. When he is unable to retake the city, he retreats through Utrecht and **Rotterdam**, where he allows his troops to massacre innocent citizens. **Flushing**, a city on **Walcheren Island** near the mouth of the **Scheldt (Schelde) River**, is the second city to declare independence from Spain. Then the city of **Mons (Bergen)** is liberated by Count Louis. Representatives of the states of Holland meet in **Dort (Dordrecht)** and declare allegiance to the Prince of Orange. The prince, marching toward Mons, crosses the **Rhine River** and passes through **Mechlin** before he is forced to turn back. Later, Captain Martin sails through the **Zuider (Zuyder) Zee** on his way to **Amsterdam**, which is still loyal to Spain.

Read Chapter III

☐ What action do the sailors aboard the *Good Venture* take when they hear of the danger to Captain Martin?

☐ What is an arquebuse? What is a pike?

☐ Captain Martin tries to slip away without fighting. How does his unwanted confrontation with the Spanish begin?

☐ How does Captain Martin trick the Spanish during the sea battle?

☐ What happens to Captain Martin in the battle?

Think It Over

The sailors aboard the *Good Venture* tell Captain Martin, "What happens to you happens to all of us" (see page 41/42). What does that reveal about Captain Martin's character? In what ways does Captain Martin demonstrate good leadership in this chapter?

Vocabulary

Find how each of the words listed below is used in Chapter III. Using the context as your cue, write down what you think each word means. Now look up the words in the dictionary to see if you are right, and if not, correct your definition.

repulsed	page 47/49
ascended	page 49/51
flurry	page 53/55
elevate	page 54/56
eluded	page 57/59

Activities

- Reread the description of the sea battle on pages 50-55/53-57. Use the diagram on page 14 of this study guide to help you picture the ships' maneuvers.

- Find the following places on the map on page 66 of this study guide: The *Good Venture* slips out of **Amsterdam** into the **Zuider (Zuyder) Zee**, clashes with the Spanish ship, and then runs to **Enkhuizen**.

Read Chapter IV

☐ How do the people of Enkhuizen receive the news that the *Good Venture* has exchanged fire with a Spanish ship?

☐ What do the doctors do about Captain Martin's leg?

☐ What is First Mate Peters' plan?

☐ How are the Catholics in the cities that were loyal to the prince to be treated, according to his orders?

Think It Over

What advice does Captain Martin give Ned with regard to conducting business honorably (see page 71-72/74-75)? How could you apply Captain Martin's counsel to your own life right now?

Vocabulary

Use the following words from Chapter IV to complete the sentences below.

imperative	page 58/60
indignation	page 61/64
distraught	page 66/69
tedious	page 68/71
inferred	page 69/72

It is absolutely _____ that I get to the airport by five o'clock!

I had never seen her so _____ as when her dog died.

The _____ minutes tick by slowly when I am pulling weeds in the garden.

We were filled with _____ when we saw the animals being mistreated.

I _____ from his remark that he did not like the movie.

Activities

- Read **The Low Countries**, beginning on page 15 of this guide, and put the most important events on the timeline below.

0   100   200   300   400

400   500   600   700   800

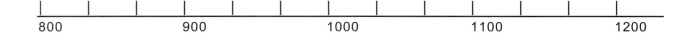

800   900   1000   1100   1200

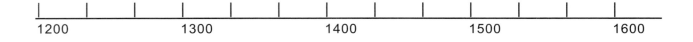

1200   1300   1400   1500   1600

1600   1700   1800   1900   2000

Vocabulary Words from the Preface and Chapters I through IV

ascended	elevate	imperative	repulsed
assent	eluded	indignation	ribald
beleaguered	facsimile	inferred	sanguine
bigot	flurry	maritime	somber
canon	heretic	mercenaries	sublime
clement	imbued	rendezvous	tedious
distraught			

Review

In some of the following sentences, the vocabulary word (in **bold** type) is not used correctly. Decide whether each sentence is correct or incorrect, and circle the sentence number of those that you believe are incorrect.

1. He **ascended** to the conditions of the contract, even though he thought some of them were not in his own best interests.

2. As he began the **assent**, he looked up one last time, fixing in his mind the route he would take to the top.

3. **Beleaguered** by the toddlers' constant demands, he vowed never to help in the nursery again.

4. Abraham **bigot** Isaac, and Isaac **bigot** Jacob.

5. The Spaniards' **canon** fired suddenly, but the shot was high, and no harm was done.

6. He was **distraught** over the loss of his favorite picture of the two of them together.

7. As the battleship continued to shell the island, the gun became so hot that the aiming mechanism failed, making it impossible to **elevate** the gun enough to strike the enemy's position.

8. He **eluded** to an earlier conversation we had had, but I had no recollection of it.

9. You don't have to send me the original, a **facsimile** will do fine.

10. The gray sky and drizzling rain gave a **somber** feel to the day.

11. Joan of Arc was burned as a **heretic**, but the motive behind her execution was political, not doctrinal.

12. He **imbued** the drink slowly, so that he could savor its flavor as long as possible.

13. An **imperative** sentence is one that issues a command.

14. The **indignation** I felt at this insult was overwhelming—I had to say something.

15. His remarks **inferred** that I had been negligent, which was absolutely untrue.

16. Mother Teresa and the nuns of her order were **mercenaries** to the poor living on the brutal streets of Calcutta.

17. I will **rendezvous** you on your cell phone tonight around ten o'clock.

18. I was **repulsed** by his arrogance.

19. To me, the Alps possess a **sublime** beauty found nowhere else in the world.

20. The **tedious** look on his face reflected the tension and anxiety of the last few hours.

Scoring

Now check your answers on page 70 of this guide. How many did you get right?

19-20	WOW!
17-18	Very good—you really know these words!
15-16	Not too bad!
13-14	Were you paying attention when you did the vocabulary exercises?
11-12	You were guessing, weren't you?

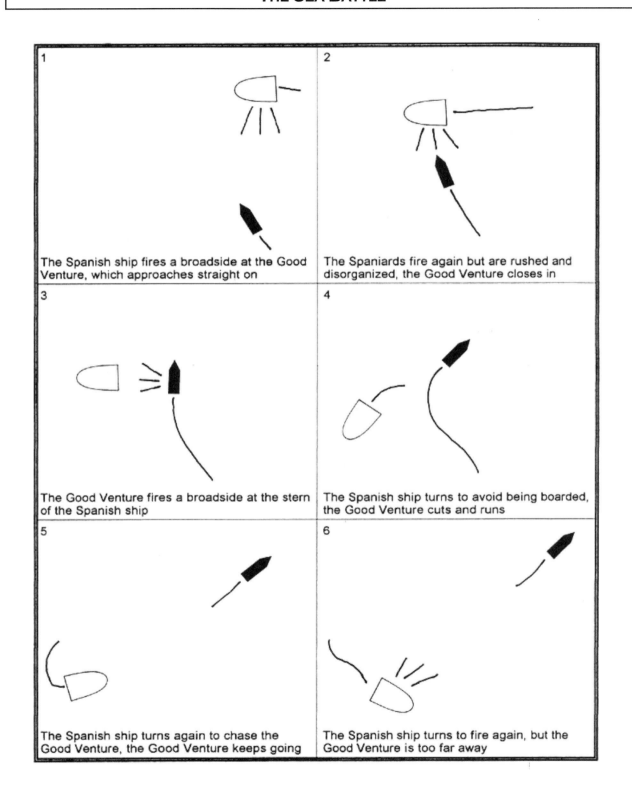

1 The Spanish ship fires a broadside at the Good Venture, which approaches straight on	**2** The Spaniards fire again but are rushed and disorganized, the Good Venture closes in
3 The Good Venture fires a broadside at the stern of the Spanish ship	**4** The Spanish ship turns to avoid being boarded, the Good Venture cuts and runs
5 The Spanish ship turns again to chase the Good Venture, the Good Venture keeps going	**6** The Spanish ship turns to fire again, but the Good Venture is too far away

Fifty-seven years before the birth of Christ, a Roman general moved his army north from Gaul (France) toward the Low Countries. He was determined to conquer this largely unknown land, and he was utterly ruthless. Most of those who resisted him, of course, he killed. But those who were especially troublesome, he left alive–with their hands cut off. Although the people of the Low Countries fought bravely, divided states could not withstand this organized, disciplined, well-equipped Roman army or the brilliant strategy of its general. Only the Frisians in the swampy northern part of the Low Countries were left alone. This conquest was not to extend the territory of Rome, not to plunder the riches of the conquered lands, not to safeguard the borders of the realm. It was to help the general gain the prestige he needed to reach a personal goal–to become the supreme ruler of the greatest empire on earth. He succeeded. He would later be known to the world as Julius Caesar.

With the Romans came 250 years of peace, prosperity, and change. Roads, forts, and temples were built. Shipping moved up and down the rivers. Traders brought merchandise from Italy and elsewhere. Soldiers came and went. All the while, the culture of Rome–language, law, learning, and religion–was taking hold. But Rome was rotten at the core, and soon the empire began to collapse in on itself. When the Roman army fell back toward Rome around 300 AD, foreign invaders moved in to fill the vacuum. The strongest of these were the Franks, who—like the Romans— conquered the Low Countries and ruled them for more than 500 years. And the history of the Low Countries was ever after bound up in the history of the church, for with the Franks came Christianity.

The Pope and The Emperor

On the day after Christmas in 795, Leo III was elected Pope of the Roman Catholic Church. But the man he was to replace, Adrian I, wasn't quite ready to retire. During a ceremonial procession, Adrian's accomplices attacked Leo and publicly accused him of crimes against the church. Adrian was planning to punish Leo for these "crimes" by blinding and maiming him, making him unable to serve as pope. Leo fled to Charlemagne, the great king of the Franks, for protection. Charlemagne provided Leo with an escort that not only took him safely back to Rome but also ousted Adrian's supporters. Soon afterwards, Charlemagne went to Rome himself to help Leo restore order. On Christmas Day, 800, the Pope was expected to consecrate Charlemagne's son in St. Peter's Cathedral before a large crowd. "Suddenly, as Charlemagne rose from prayer, Leo placed a crown on his head,"[1] knelt before him, and proclaimed him the first emperor of the Holy Roman Empire.

After Charlemagne died, the Low Countries remained part of the Holy Roman Empire. The political association between the two was fairly vague during the Middle Ages, when local nobles ruled the Low Countries without much interference from afar. Viking raids in the 800s and 900s forced people in coastal areas to strengthen the defenses of their settlements and move inside the walls. Thus settlements grew into towns and towns grew into cities. By the time of the Renaissance in the 1400s, the Low Countries had hundreds of strong, independent cities, a large middle class of merchants and craftsmen, and an active economy based on trade. The people were deeply religious, and were, of course, Catholic.

A Fine Tragedy

When the Protestant teachings of Luther and Calvin reached the Low Countries in the 1500s, they were quickly embraced, for they "seemed to suit the genius and character of the Dutch people, and to fit in with their aspirations after liberty."[2] At that time, the Low Countries were part of the vast territory of Charles V, king of Spain and emperor of the Holy Roman Empire. As Protestant beliefs began to take hold among the Dutch, Charles brought the horrors of the Inquisition to their land. Thousands were executed in a period of persecution lasting 30 years. Yet when Charles gave up his throne in 1555, Protestant doctrine was more firmly established than ever before.

With Charles' abdication, control of Spain and the Low Countries passed to his son, Philip II, and the persecution ended for a while. Then Philip began to take an interest in his new possession. In 1566 he declared that all his subjects must endorse the beliefs and practices of the Catholic Church or face the vengeance of the Inquisition. As the tension mounted in the Low Countries, Protestant rioters destroyed sacred images in the Catholic churches. Philip, outraged at this insolence and blasphemy, sent the Duke of Alva to subdue the heretics. "Now," the Prince of Orange announced, "we shall see the beginning of a fine tragedy."[3]

As Alva's tyrannical Council of Blood began to hold court, "thousands were put to death, thousands had their goods confiscated by the state, and thousands fled to England, Germany, and elsewhere."[4] A group of nobles, including the brother of the Prince of Orange, came to plead with the Spanish for religious tolerance. One of Philip's counselors dismissed them scornfully as a pack of "beggars." From then on, those who opposed Spanish rule proudly called themselves the Beggars. The simmering Dutch resistance erupted into open revolt in 1572, when the Sea Beggars seized Brielle, and William I, the Prince of Orange—also called William the Silent—took the stage to play out his role in this fine tragedy.

Ahead of Its Time

In 1579 the northern states of the Low Countries overcame their reluctance to work together, and formed an alliance called the Union of Utrecht to oppose the Spanish. These northern states, mostly Protestant, would later become the country we call the Netherlands while the southern states, mostly Catholic, would become Belgium. Two years later, the northern states formally declared their independence from Spain. Philip, unable to crush the rebellion outright, offered a reward of 25,000 gold crowns for the Prince of Orange, dead or alive. In 1584, the prince was assassinated. Dutch resistance faltered briefly, but England finally joined the fight and, in 1588, destroyed the Spanish Armada. By the end of the century, all Spanish troops had withdrawn from the northern states. Although a truce was signed, war broke out again. A treaty recognizing the Dutch Republic as a sovereign state was not ratified until 1648.

The Dutch Republic now entered a period of prosperity, exploration, colonization, and cultural advancement known as the Golden Age, and became one of the most prominent and powerful nations in Europe. As a republic (a government with power invested in representatives of the people) rather than a monarchy (a government ruled by a king or queen whose position is hereditary) it was ahead of its time. Despite internal disputes over the issue of predestination, and wars with England and France, this was the zenith of Dutch history. But it didn't last very long. In the 1700s, Dutch influence began to fade as England and France grew stronger.

The Nation of the Netherlands

Napoleon annexed the Dutch Republic to the French Empire in 1810. During the reorganization of European boundaries that followed Napoleon's fall, the republic was reunited with Belgium in an unhappy and short-lived marriage. Belgium rebelled, the maps were revised again, and the nation of the Netherlands as it is known today emerged in 1839.

The Netherlands was a prosperous nation when World War I began, and the Dutch, wanting to stay out of the conflict, declared neutrality. Nevertheless they were hurt badly by the war, for when the Allies blockaded Europe, the Dutch lost their major source of income—international trade. They were hit a second time by the world-wide depression of the 1930's, and a third time by World War II, which began in 1939. Although the Netherlands once again declared neutrality, Germany bombed Rotterdam into ruins, invaded the country, and occupied it until 1945. Much of the Netherlands was destroyed by the Germans, by Allied attacks on German positions, and by the Dutch themselves, who, just as they did in the time of the Prince of Orange, opened the dikes and flooded the land to hinder their enemies.

In the last half-century, the people of the Netherlands have worked to build a modern nation with a stable government and a thriving international economy.

1   Barraclough, G. (2000). Holy Roman Empire. In *Encyclopedia Britannica Online*. Retrieved June 13, 2000 from the World Wide Web: http://eb.com:180/bol/topic?eu=109232&sctn=5
2   Houghton, S. (1980). *Sketches from Church History*. Carlisle, PA: Banner of Truth Trust, p. 138.
3   Houghton, S. (1980). *Sketches from Church History*. Carlisle, PA: Banner of Truth Trust, p. 141.
4   Ibid.

Read Chapter V

☐ Who arrives in Enkhuizen on the *Good Venture*?

☐ What does Ned resolve to do?

☐ How does Ned's mother react to his decision?

☐ How does Ned's father react to his decision?

Think It Over

Ned explains his decision to join the Prince of Orange and fight against the Spaniards on pages 86-87/92-93. How does he justify this decision? Do you think his reasons are valid?

Vocabulary

The following words are found in Chapter V. The definitions are provided for you. Write one paragraph (or if you really like a challenge, one sentence) that uses all five words correctly and still makes sense.

agitation – excitement   page 77/81
parley – discussion   page 82/88
prostrate – exhausted   page 85/90
meddle – interfere   page 88/94
embark – begin   page 89/95

Activities

- First Mate Peters tells Ned, "...never again will John Peters undertake a job where he is got to keep his mouth shut when a woman wants to get something out of him. Lor' bless you, lad, they just see right through you; and you feel that, twist and turn as you will, they will get it out of you sooner or later" (see page 84/89). Just for fun, ask several people—male and female, young and old—these questions: Do women have more insight than men do? Are women better able to tell when someone is lying than men are? How *do* you tell when someone is lying?

Read Chapter VI

☐ Why does Captain Martin give Ned his permission to join the prince?

☐ What does Captain Martin mean when he says, "There is none of the chivalry of past times in the struggle here"?

☐ What is Captain Martin's final advice to Ned? Is it wise?

☐ How does the prince come to be called William the Silent?

Think It Over

Ned decides that "there is honor and glory in the struggle" of the Netherlands against Spain (see page 98/105). Do you agree? Why or why not?

Reread Captain Martin's description of the state of affairs in the Netherlands (see pages 95/101-102 and 101-102/109). Why would the people of the Netherlands "have no thought of throwing off their allegiance to Spain, if Spain will but be tolerant" after all they had suffered? Why are the different states of the Netherlands so reluctant to join together? What do you think about this? Do you think the same kind of thing could happen in our country today? Why or why not?

Vocabulary

Find the following words in Chapter VI, and using the context as your cue, match each word to its definition.

demeanor	page 92/98
subdued	page 93/99
presumptuous	page 95/101
abjure	page 95/102
reticence	page 103/111

renounce; abandon
arrogant
manner; way of behaving
tendency to be quiet and reserved
inactive; dispirited

Activities

- **Write and Save**–Using the information presented in pages 102-106/110-115, write a summary of the life of the Prince of Orange. Now describe his character and abilities: what kind of a man was he, and how do you know? Give evidence for each trait you list.

- Ned sails from **Enkhuizen** to **Rotterdam** to meet the prince. Trace his voyage on the map on page 66 of this guide.

Read Chapter VII

☐ What does the prince decide to do with Ned?

☐ Who does Ned go to see in Haarlem, and what is the outcome of his visit?

☐ What dangerous mission does the prince entrust to Ned?

☐ Why is Ned told to meet a man in a blue cap?

☐ Why is trade still going on between Dutch cities that had rebelled and those that are under Spanish control?

☐ How do the Spanish soldiers support themselves, since their pay is always in arrears, and what effect does this have on the Dutch economy?

☐ Who does Ned meet on the road to Brussels, and what is Ned commanded to do?

Think It Over

Reread Ned's conversation with his aunt on pages 113-114/119-121. Ned argues that his aunt should flee to England for safety, but his aunt doesn't want to go. What are her arguments? Do they sound logical to you? Why won't Ned's aunt face the fact that staying in Haarlem could be disastrous? Why do people sometimes think and act illogically in situations such as this?

Analyze Ned's conversation with Von Aert on pages 119-121/126-128. Does Ned lie? Would lying be justified in this situation? Is lying ever justified?

Vocabulary

Use the following words from Chapter VII to complete the sentences below.

countenance	page 108/115
omen	page 108/115
disdain	page 108/116
discreetly	page 110/117
corroborate	page 119/126

It seems to me to be a bad _____ that the president would even _____ such a dangerous plan.

If you don't think I'm telling the truth, ask Erin. She will _____ my story.

She has always treated me with _____ ; she seems to think she is better than everyone else.

You must talk very _____ about these things; there are some who would misuse this knowledge.

Activities

- **Write and Save**—In this chapter a great deal is revealed about the character of the Prince of Orange. Make a list of things you notice about the prince—the way he treats Ned, the sort of court he maintains, the mission he gives Ned—and describe the character trait each item on your list illustrates.

- Ned travels from **Rotterdam** to **Brussels**—by ship out into the North Sea, then around the southern tip of **Walcheren Island**, and by land to **Axel**, then **Antwerp**, and then **Brussels**. Trace his journey on the map on page 66 of this guide.

Read Chapter VIII

☐ What does Ned learn about Von Aert from the innkeeper's wife?

☐ What does Ned learn about the situation in Brussels from the innkeeper's wife?

☐ How is Ned caught by Von Aert?

☐ What does the council decide to do with Ned, and why?

☐ What is Ned's plan? What does he intend to do if he is caught trying to escape?

Think It Over

Reread what the weaver tells Ned, and what Ned thinks about it, on pages 128-129/135-137. Why do you think so many people of the Netherlands feel the same way the weaver does about rebelling against Spain, though the Spaniards' tyranny grows continually worse?

Ned realizes that Von Aert's promise to release him "means absolutely nothing–the Spaniards having no hesitation in breaking the most solemn oaths made to heretics" (see page 134/143). What do you think about this? Is breaking a promise ever justified? What if you make a very foolish promise?

Vocabulary

The following words are taken from Chapter VIII. Find each word and, using the context as your cue, write down what you think it means. Now look up the words in the dictionary to see if you are right, and if not, correct your definition.

rites	page 125/133
subsidy	page 128/136
malicious	page 129/137
abject	page 132/140
allusion	page 135/143

Activities

- Find out more about the Spanish Inquisition.

- When Ned encounters Von Aert on the road from **Axel** to **Antwerp**, he detours to the city of **Ghent**, crosses the **Scheldt (Schelde) River**, and then proceeds to **Brussels**, which is in the province of **Brabant**. Trace his journey on the map on page 66 of this guide.

Read Chapter IX

- ☐ What are some of the very improbable things that happen in this chapter?

- ☐ What causes Ned to choose the house he entered, and why is he so bold in telling the occupants about his predicament?

- ☐ What reason does the countess give for not fearing the risks involved in hiding Ned?

- ☐ Although the men of Brussels are ripe for a revolt, they need something to get them started. What do they need?

- ☐ One of the men to whom Ned delivers a letter says that one thing holds the provinces back from working together in a united way. What is that one thing and what is the prince's position concerning it?

- ☐ How does Ned get to speak to the Count of Sluys?

Think It Over

On page 151/162, Ned says, "But in religion as in all other things, men will differ just as they do about the meats they eat and the wines they drink." What do you think about this? What sorts of things do different Christian denominations argue about today? Is it all right for Christians to disagree about these things? What beliefs are not negotiable for Christians? Do you think religious unity is possible in the modern Christian community? If so, how could it be achieved, and what would it look like? Think about the Catholic Church's insistence on religious conformity in the Netherlands during the time of the Prince of Orange. Are there any ways that a movement promoting religious unity could be dangerous today, as it was then?

Also on page 151/161, the prince's insistence on "absolute toleration of all religions" is mentioned. Religious freedom is granted to Unites States citizens by the Bill of Rights, which says, "Congress shall make no law respecting an establishment of religion, or prohibiting the free exercise thereof." What do you think the relationship between the government and the church should be like? Are there any ways in which you see an improper relationship between the government and the church in the United States today?

Vocabulary

Use the following words from Chapter IX to complete the sentences below.

abstained   page 138/147
inadvertently   page 142/151
metamorphosis   page 145/154
minions   page 147/157
voluble   page 152/163

The _____ was complete: he was no longer a boy, he was a man.

The duke _____ gave him the wrong packet.

He could not decide whether to vote yes or no, so he _____ .

In spite of her _____ protests, no one paid any attention to her.

The evil king and his _____ brought death and destruction to the land.

Activities

- Just for fun, imagine that you have to go about in your own community without being recognized. What sort of a disguise would you devise? If your parents are willing, go ahead and put your disguise together and try it out.

Vocabulary Words from Chapters V through IX

abject	demeanor	meddle	prostrate
abjure	discreetly	metamorphosis	reticence
abstained	disdain	minions	rites
agitation	embark	omen	subdued
allusion	inadvertently	parley	subsidy
corroborate	malicious	presumptuous	voluble
countenance			

Review

Use the words listed above to complete the crossword puzzle on the next page. The clues are given below. Check your answers on page 70 of this guide.

	Across		Down
1	transformation	1	interfere
6	begin	2	wretched, obsequious
7	behavior, deportment	3	suppressed
8	despise, disregard	4	allowance
9	renounce, forsake	5	not given to speaking freely
12	permit, endorse	9	refrained from voting
13	excitement, uneasiness	10	prone, exhausted
15	reference	11	spiteful, vicious
16	unintentionally	14	ceremonies
18	sign, premonition	17	loud
20	audacious, brazen	19	subordinates
21	confirm	20	discussion
22	cautiously, secretly		

The Kingdom of the Netherlands is a very modern and prosperous country today. It is also a socialized country, which means that the government assumes responsibility for many of the needs people may have. Education and health care are provided by the government, and people who are unemployed, old, disabled, or widowed receive financial help. Families are given an allowance for children, and many people live in subsidized housing. Much of the national budget is spent on programs like these, for the system of social welfare in the Netherlands is quite elaborate. The United States, of course, has social welfare programs, too. One of the political issues about which people disagree today is whether our country should be more socialized than it is now, that is, whether it should be more like the Netherlands.

Land in the Netherlands is scarce, as it always has been, and the country is very crowded. The average number of people per square mile in the United States is 75. In the Netherlands, it is 1200. Most people live in the larger cities, where there is a chronic housing shortage. Although the population is growing slowly, because the birth rate is low, there are more and more people who are elderly, because the death rate is low, too. Elderly people receive a large share of the money allocated by the government for welfare programs because they do not work, they are often disabled and widowed, and they usually need more health care than younger people do.

During the time of the Prince of Orange, the people of the Netherlands were deeply religious. This is no longer true. Churches and Christians are increasingly excluded from Dutch public life, because "steady secularization and anti-discrimination legislation threaten Christian liberties in the name of tolerance."[1] Dutch society "has turned its back on its past" and has become a society "with few restrictions on drugs, deviant life styles, prostitution, homosexuality, abortion, and euthanasia."[2]

The Keys of Death

Euthanasia, sometimes called "mercy killing," means deliberately putting sick people to death as a way of releasing them from their suffering. In 1993, the Netherlands created an international uproar by becoming the first country in the world (not counting Nazi Germany) to formally permit doctors to practice euthanasia. Although euthanasia was still technically illegal, doctors were told that they would not be held responsible if they followed certain guidelines. For example, patients could be put to death only if they made a voluntary and informed request to die. In 2000, the Netherlands made euthanasia completely legal, as long as doctors followed the official guidelines.

Many doctors, however, paid little attention to the guidelines. In 1995, Dutch doctors reported ending or shortening the lives of 24,500 patients (it is generally believed that many more cases were not reported). The doctors admitted that more than 15,000 of these people did not ask to die–they were put to death without their consent. Some of them–disabled infants, psychiatric patients, and elderly people who had lost their mental abilities–could not possibly have requested euthanasia.[3]

The Light of the World

In every society, there are people who are sick or dying. There are people who are mentally or physically handicapped. There are people–young and old–whose families don't really want them. There are people who are depressed or mentally ill. There are people who can't work or whose needs are expensive. Without the influence of Christian principles in a society, these people can become a "problem" and euthanasia can become a "solution." A person's worth becomes defined by what is usually called the "quality" of that person's life. At first, the quality of life is decided by each individual, and a life is considered worth living if someone can enjoy work and play and relationships with others, is free from suffering, and is happy. But once a society accepts this definition of human worth, especially if it is a socialized society, a person's right to live may come to be determined by others–someone may be considered to be worth keeping alive only if the person is useful or desirable to the community in some way. This is apparently what has happened in the Netherlands.

Christian principles affirm that God gives us life. He numbers our days and fills them according to his own will, which we cannot always understand. We live not for our own happiness but for his glory, and if we should suffer, our suffering has meaning and purpose. We are to respect those who are weak, care for those who are helpless, put others' needs above our own, and recognize the dignity of every person. We are not to kill–ourselves or others–even in the name of mercy. Scripture says, " . . . choose life, so that you and your children may live and that you may love the Lord your God, listen to his voice, and hold fast to him" (Deuteronomy 30:19-20).

---

[1] Johnstone, P. (1993) *Operation World*. Grand Rapids, MI: Zondervan, p. 408.
[2] Ibid., p. 409.
[3] Jochemsen, H. & Keown, J. (1999). Voluntary euthanasia under control? Further empirical evidence from the Netherlands. *Journal of Medical Ethics, 25* (1), p. 16-22.

Read Chapter X

- ☐ How does Ned get the last letter to its recipient?

- ☐ How does the Count of Sluys help Ned?

- ☐ What do the Spanish soldiers do to the cities of Mechlin and Zutphen and their inhabitants? What is the effect of this on the people of the Netherlands?

- ☐ Who does Ned encounter in Antwerp and how does he escape from him?

- ☐ What happens at the inn?

Think It Over

In this chapter the Spanish believe that they are faithful Christians ridding the world of heretics in obedience to God's will. What in their actions is inconsistent with this belief?

Reread the conversation between Ned and the landlord of the inn on pages 166-167/177-178. The landlord is afraid that the Spanish soldiers will ruin his business and harm his family, but he doesn't know what to do. Ned discourages him from poisoning the soldiers, and advises him to escape to Holland, but the landlord is too afraid. What would you do in this situation?

Vocabulary

Find the following words in Chapter X, and using the context as your cue, match each word to its definition.

procure	page 156/166
desecration	page 161/170
effigy	page 161/170
listlessly	page 161/171
pestilent	page 163/173

image; likeness
obtain; acquire
troublesome; causing vexation
sluggishly; apathetically
treating something holy in a profane or sacrilegious way

Activities

- Find a modern map of the Netherlands and compare it to the map on page 66 of this guide. Pay special attention to the Zuider Zee and the place where the Maas, Waal, and Rhine rivers empty into the sea. What has changed?

- Find out more about the Netherlands' battle to reclaim land from the sea. When did the Dutch begin building dikes? What role did windmills play in this battle? How much of the Netherlands today is reclaimed land?

- Just for fun, try building a small model of a windmill. Check your encyclopedia for a picture you can use as a guide.

- Ned leaves **Brussels** on the road to Antwerp, passing through **Mechlin**, where, a month before, the city had been sacked and its inhabitants slaughtered by the Spanish in retaliation for allowing the prince to enter the city. He comes to **Antwerp**, where the news of the destruction of **Zutphen (Zutphem)** has just arrived. After encountering Genet, he leaves on the road for **St. Nicholas**. Find these places on the map on page 66 of this guide.

Read Chapter XI

☐ Why does the landlord say, "Mynheer Van Bost is a Protestant and a rich man–that is quite enough for the Blood Council"?

☐ Why does Ned involve himself in Van Bost's troubles?

☐ What does "inquire into the condition of life and the probable means of each of these suspected persons" mean?

☐ What is the crime of the cloth manufacturer Ned first calls on in St. Nicholas?

☐ What sort of trial or proof is offered by the Council of Blood to justify the arrest of the cloth manufacturer?

☐ How do members of the Blood Council benefit personally by condemning a heretic?

☐ How does Ned plan to escape from Bergen-op-Zoom?

Think It Over

Ned kills Genet but has "not a shadow of compunction" about Genet's fate (see page 172/183). Ned doesn't feel guilty about this because he believes that he has done nothing wrong. (Has he?) Sometimes we too believe we have done nothing wrong because we don't feel guilty. Where do guilt feelings come from? What is their purpose? Can guilt feelings–or the lack of them–lead us astray? How can we know for certain whether something is right or wrong?

In what ways is the Spaniards' system of justice unjust (see pages 176-177/188-189)? How does the system of justice in the Unites States today protect the rights of the accused? (Look up the Bill of Rights in an encyclopedia.) Are any aspects of our system of justice derived from biblical principles?

Vocabulary

Use the following words from Chapter XI to complete the sentences below.

baffle   page 170/181
compunction   page 172/183
confiscation   page 176/188
pompous   page 176/188
stupefied   page 177/190

Child-proof caps always _____ me. Will you please help me open this bottle?

He is a _____ , vain, boorish know-it-all.

I have no _____ whatsoever about what I did–it was the only thing I could have done under the circumstances.

The news that the bus had gone without him left him utterly _____ .

_____ of private property by the police is allowed in certain circumstances, such as when that property has been used in illegal activities.

Activities

- Find out more about the Netherlands today. In the Netherlands today, where is the longest dike? Where are the largest polders? What is reclaimed land used for? Are there any large cities on reclaimed land? What happened in the Netherlands on February 1, 1953?

- The papers Ned takes from Genet allow him to warn people in **St. Nicholas**, (and allows *them* to warn people in **Sluys** and **Axel**) that they are suspected of heresy by the Blood Council. After leaving St. Nicholas, he travels on to **Bergen-op-Zoom**. Find these places on the map on page 66 of this guide.

Read Chapter XII

☐ What happens as Ned and the others are drifting down the river to escape from Bergen-Op-Zoom?

☐ How is Ned received by the prince?

☐ The prince tells his advisors about Ned's abilities (see pages 198-199). How does he describe Ned?

☐ What happens at Naarden? How were the people of the Netherlands affected by Naarden's destruction?

☐ How does Ned end up on board the *Good Venture* again?

☐ What happens at the very end of this chapter?

Think It Over

On page 197/210, the prince describes the dilemma he faces. What is this dilemma? What do you think he should do?

The Spaniards announced that "the deliberate policy of the government" was "that every man, woman, and child would be exterminated in every city which opposed the Spanish authority" (see page 201/214). What were they really trying to accomplish by this policy? In what ways is this policy similar to terrorism today? What do you think is the best way to fight terrorists?

Vocabulary

The following words are found in Chapter XII. The definitions are provided for you. Write one paragraph (or if you really like a challenge, one sentence) that uses all five words correctly and still makes sense.

incredulous – surprised, doubtful	page 193/207
aver – declare, affirm	page 199/212
cordial – friendly, warm	page 199/212
deputation – delegation, group of people representing others	page 200/213
sumptuous – extravagant, lavish	page 200/213

Activities

- In the time of the Prince of Orange, sea trade was the heart of the Netherlands' economy. Using an encyclopedia, find out more about the economy of the Netherlands today. What role does international trade and finance play in the economy now? What about industry and agriculture? What things must the Netherlands buy from other countries (imports)? What things do they sell to other countries (exports)?

- Ned sails from **Bergen-op-Zoom** straight out through the islands on the east side of **Walcheren Island** to the open sea, and then around to **Rotterdam**. After meeting the prince in Rotterdam, he sails on the *Good Venture* around to the **Zuider (Zuyder) Zee**, and up to the "mouth of the strait leading from the **Zuider Zee** to **Haarlem**." There he is trapped in the ice in full view of the Spanish army in **Amsterdam**. Find these places on the map on page 66 of this guide.

- Look at the map on page 66 of this guide and see what Captain Martin means when he says that by capturing **Haarlem**, the Spaniards would cut the province of **Holland** in two.

Read Chapter XIII

☐ How did the Sea Beggars hold off the Spanish when frozen in the ice?

☐ What was the situation in Haarlem when Ned arrived?

☐ What happened to the two groups of reinforcements that the prince sent?

☐ Why did the prince relieve De la Marck of his command?

☐ How did the women of Haarlem help in the fight?

☐ What was Ned's plan to make his cousins safe should the city fall?

Think It Over

Atrocities such as those described on page 216/231 seem to occur in every war. Why is this? What can make people, who otherwise seem perfectly normal, commit barbarous acts of cruelty in time of war? What does this say about human nature?

Whether or not women should participate in combat, as they did in Haarlem, is a controversial issue in the United States today. What do you think about this issue—should women serve in combat units in the military? Why or why not?

Vocabulary

Find the following words in Chapter XIII and, using the context as your clue, write down what you think each word means. now look up the words in the dictionary to see if you are right, and if not, correct your definition.

doggedly   page 208/222
phlegmatic   page 211/226
placidly   page 211/226
portly   page 211/226
dexterously   page 214/229

Now decide which vocabulary word would be best to describe:
    someone's figure
    someone's personality
    the way someone works at a discouraging task
    when someone works at a task with skill and coordination
    how someone might react to a bit of unpleasant news

Activities

- Just for fun, go ice skating (if possible) with your family.

- The Netherlands is known for dikes, windmills, wooden shoes (*klompen*), and tulips. Find out more about tulips. When were they introduced into the Netherlands, and why, and by whom? What was the "tulip mania" of the 1630s? What was the highest price ever paid for a single tulip bulb?

- Just for fun, buy tulip bulbs and plant them in your yard or in a large flower pot.

- Look at the map on page 66 of this guide as you reread the description of **Amsterdam** and **Haarlem** on page 209/223-224.

Read Chapter XIV

☐ Why does Don Frederick decide to starve the people of Haarlem into submission?

☐ Why does Don Frederick ask permission to end the siege of Haarlem, and how does Alva respond to his request?

☐ What is the purpose of the mission the prince entrusts to Sonoy?

☐ Why do the people of Haarlem despair when they see the Spaniards defeat the Dutch fleet in the lake?

☐ Why does Batenburg's attempt to relieve Haarlem fail?

☐ How do the Spaniards treat the people of Haarlem after capturing the city?

Think It Over

Reread the description of Captain Curey on pages 228-229/243-244. This man has a natural "horror of bloodshed" and is "ill with remorse" after each battle. What enables him and the people of Haarlem to fight so courageously?

The people of Haarlem know very well that the Spaniards did not keep their promises of mercy to other Dutch cities that had surrendered. Why then do they surrender?

Vocabulary

Read these (rather silly) sentences:

I implore you to give me succor! My job is so monotonous, it induces so much boredom, that I can't wait for the cessation of work each day.

Now rewrite the sentences so that the overall meaning is preserved, **without** using the vocabulary words from Chapter XIV listed below.

cessation	page 224/239
succor	page 224/240
monotonous	page 225/240
induce	page 227/242
implore	page 235/251

Activities

- Using an encyclopedia, find out more about the government of the Netherlands today. What sort of government does the Netherlands have? What is the role of the monarch? What is the role of the States General? How is the government of the Netherlands similar to and different from ours? What problems is the government of the Netherlands experiencing today?

- Look at the map of the city of **Haarlem** on page 68 of this guide.

Read Chapter XV

☐ Why are the Spanish and German soldiers outside the walls of Haarlem so undisciplined and mutinous?

☐ Why does Alva try to win back the people of the Netherlands by persuasion? Does it work?

☐ What is the purpose of Ned's mission to Alkmaar?

☐ What is the disagreement between the Alkmaar magistrates and governor Sonoy?

☐ What is the gist of Ned's speech? How do the people of Alkmaar respond?

☐ What does Alva tell the king he intends to do to the people of Alkmaar?

Think It Over

Reread Alva's proclamation on pages 241-242/256-257. He uses biblical language—assuring the "prodigals" that their "sins" will be "forgiven and forgotten" if they will only "repent." He also warns them that they will face punishment if they "disregard these offers of mercy." How is Alva's proclamation similar to and different from God's provision for the forgiveness of sins as it is presented in the Bible?

When Ned is promoted, he wonders if he should tell the prince how young he really is (see page 246/261-262). He decides, in the end, not to do so. What do you think about this? Should Ned have corrected the prince's incorrect assumption? Is it dishonest to let someone believe something about you that is not true?

Vocabulary

Find the following words in Chapter XV, and using the context as your cue, match each word to its definition.

indefatigable   page 242/257
deride   page 243/259
diffident   page 248/265
fervor   page 252/268
clemency   page 254/271

shy; timid
compassion; mercy
tireless
enthusiasm; zeal
mock; ridicule

Activities

- The official language of the Netherlands is Dutch. Just for fun, find out more about the Dutch language. "Hallo, hoe gaat het?" means "Hello, how are you?" in Dutch. See if you can find out how to say other familiar expressions in Dutch. (Try the *www.learndutch.org* website.)

- Some English words, such as *skate* and *yacht*, are derived from Dutch. See if you can find more. (Try the *dictionaries.travlang.com/englishdutch* website.)

- Ned slips out of **Haarlem** and goes to **Leyden** and then to **Delft**, where he finds the prince. The prince sends him to **Alkmaar**. Find these places on the map on page 66 of this guide.

Vocabulary Words from Chapters X to XV

aver	cordial	doggedly	induce	pompous
baffle	deputation	effigy	listlessly	portly
cessation	deride	fervor	monotonous	procure
clemency	desecration	implored	pestilent	stupefied
compunction	dexterously	incredulous	phlegmatic	succor
confiscation	diffident	indefatigable	placidly	sumptuous

Review

In some of the following sentences, the vocabulary word (in **bold** type) is not used correctly. Decide whether each sentence is correct or incorrect, and circle the sentence number of those that you believe are incorrect.

1. Many people feel compelled to **aver** the scene of an unpleasant experience.

2. When we selected our campsite on the top of the mountain, we didn't realize that the wind would **baffle** us all night long, making sleep nearly impossible.

3. The whispering **cessation** of the leaves blowing in the gentle breeze lulled us to sleep.

4. I know it was wrong, but I felt little **compunction** about the way I had treated her–after all, she had treated me exactly the same way.

5. He didn't exactly lie, but his answer was so roundabout and ambiguous that he succeeded in producing a thorough **confiscation** of the truth.

6. Some people believe that the professionalization of the Olympics that has occurred in the last twenty years is a **desecration** of the original ideals of the games.

7. I could tell he was deeply offended–his flushing face, his **diffident** sniff, and his narrowed eyes gave his feelings away.

8. In the Iditarod, you must either race **doggedly** or lose.

9. The **fervor** that some people show for professional wrestling is a little scary.

10. The pressure on the hull of the submarine was so great that at last it simply **implored**.

11. My sister is so **incredulous** that she will believe almost anything I say.

12. If you think about the facts carefully, you can **induce** that the butler could not have done it.

13. Although he was small in size, he was **indefatigable**–I never saw anyone work as hard as he did!

14. He always forgot half of the things he needed when he went to the store **listlessly**.

15. People used to believe that the night air was **pestilent**–they didn't understand how diseases like malaria were spread.

16. His personality is so **phlegmatic** that absolutely nothing upsets him.

17. I would have been very upset, but he just walked **placidly** away.

18. It is often true that the most **pompous** people you meet have the least reason to be proud.

19. His job was to **procure** the necessary materials to fabricate the machine.

20. The ground was so saturated with water that it was too **sumptuous** to walk on without sinking into the mud.

Scoring

Now check your answers on page 71 of this guide. How many did you get right?

19-20	WOW!
17-18	Very good–you really know these words!
15-16	Not too bad!
13-14	Were you paying attention when you did the vocabulary exercises?
11-12	You were guessing, weren't you?

The Prince of Orange never saw his country free from the tyranny of Spain. And when he died, few people would have believed that the tiny Netherlands could ever resist "the greatest power of the time." By 1650, however, the Dutch had not only won their independence, but they had grown into the world's leading sea power. The Netherlands had twice as many ships as England and France combined, more than half of the world's shipping travelled in Dutch vessels, and Amsterdam was the most important center of commerce in Europe. There were Dutch colonies and trading posts in Brazil, the Caribbean islands, South Africa, Indonesia, and, of course, on Manhattan Island. This busy international trade gave the Dutch the highest standard of living in Europe and brought them into contact with people–and their ideas–from all over the world. National independence, economic prosperity, and lively cultural exchange combined to make the 1600's the Dutch Golden Age. It was a time of remarkable advancements in science, philosophy, literature, and especially, art.

In medieval Europe, master artists painted mostly for kings and cathedrals. One result of the economic changes during the Renaissance, however, was that many people had the resources to purchase art. In the Netherlands, especially, wealthy merchants could afford to buy paintings to beautify their own homes. Art thrived because there were more private individuals (patrons) to support artists, and changed because these patrons of art typically wanted paintings of familiar things. Frans Hals painted portraits of ordinary Dutch people. Jacob van Ruisdael painted landscapes. Jan Vermeer painted pictures of everyday life: a music lesson, a girl reading a letter, a woman flirting with a soldier. These–and many others of the Dutch Golden Age–were wonderful artists, but the greatest of all was Rembrandt.

One of the Most Famous Painters

In 1641, Jan Orlers–a one-man historical society and tourist information bureau– published the second edition of his book, *A Description of the City of Leiden*. One brief entry in this book said just about everything known about Rembrandt's early life. (As you read it, notice how Orlers seemed to be disappointed that Rembrandt became an artist instead of getting a "real job.")

> Rembrandt van Rijn…was born in the city of Leiden on July 15, 1606. His parents sent him to school with the idea of teaching him Latin and then bringing him to the Leiden Academy. That way, when he grew up he could use his knowledge for the service of this city and the benefit of the community at large. But he hadn't the least urge or inclination in that direction, his natural bent being for painting and drawing only. His parents had no choice but to take him out of school and, in accordance with his wishes, apprentice him to a painter who would teach him the basics. Once having made up their minds,

they brought him to the able painter Jacob Isaacz. van Swanenburg for training and instruction. He stayed with him for about three years, during which time his great progress impressed art-lovers tremendously. Everyone was certain that he was going to develop into an outstanding painter. For that reason his father consented to have him taken to the famous painter [Pieter Lastman], who lived in Amsterdam, to receive more advanced and better training and instruction. After about six months with him, he decided to practice painting on his own.[1]

The truth was, after only six months, Rembrandt had surpassed his teacher. At the age of 18 or 19, he was already a master painter himself. In time his fame became too great for Leiden, and he returned to Amsterdam. Orlers called Rembrandt "one of the most famous painters"[2] of his time, but he is far more than that—he is considered one of the greatest artists of all time. What makes Rembrandt so special? What is so unique about his art?

The Greatest and Most Natural Emotion

Rembrandt painted the same subjects as other artists of his day—portraits, mythological and biblical paintings, landscapes, everyday scenes. His paintings, however, were different in a way that is hard to describe. Part of the difference had to do with technique. Rembrandt was a master at using light and shadow—called **chiaroscuro**—to make his paintings dramatic or haunting or poignant. He developed a way of layering on different thicknesses of paint that has never been matched. Every element of his paintings was finely balanced and elegantly composed. Although his style was realistic, Rembrandt's technique gave his paintings an ethereal beauty.

There was, however, something more than technique involved. Rembrandt said that he wanted to depict people "with the greatest and most natural emotion and animation."[3] Somehow, he could capture the subtlety and depth of human emotions in the facial expressions and gestures of the people he painted. It was this quality more than anything else that made his paintings so powerful and moving.

To understand what I mean, find a way to see Rembrandt's paintings for yourself. Get a book about Rembrandt from the library, or go to the internet WebMuseum at *metalab.unc.edu/wm/paint/auth/rembrandt* [4] or the Artchive at *www.artchive.com/ artchive/R/rembrandt.html*. Be sure to look at as many of Rembrandt's biblical paintings as you can. In particular, try to find his paintings of Judas returning the 30 pieces of silver, Jesus raising Lazarus from the dead, and Jesus being lowered from the cross. As you study Rembrandt's paintings, pay special attention to the faces of the people—their eyes, their mouths, their facial expressions. What are they thinking and feeling? What are *you* thinking and feeling as you look at them?

Saskia, Geertghe, and Hendrickje

When Rembrandt was 28, he married Saskia van Uylenburgh, a wealthy orphan who was related to one of his patrons. From all appearances, Rembrandt loved Saskia dearly, but their life together was not happy. Their first three children lived only weeks, and Saskia was often sick. When their fourth child, Titus, was born, Saskia was so ill that she could not take care of him. Rembrandt hired a nanny, Geertghe. Saskia died the next year, but Geertghe stayed on and soon became Rembrandt's common-law wife. He never married her (though she said he promised to) because of a provision in Saskia's will. If he remarried, the will said, Saskia's sizable inheritance would go to Titus, not to Rembrandt. By the time Titus was seven, Rembrandt had fallen in love with Hendrickje, who had joined his household sometime earlier. She was about 20, Rembrandt was 42. Geertghe, hurt and bitter, sued Rembrandt in court for support and won. So that she wouldn't have to face Rembrandt again, she sent her brother, Pieter, to collect the money for her, but he never did. He and Rembrandt conspired to produce false accusations against Geertghe and have her committed to a workhouse, where she would have no legal rights. Rembrandt kept his alimony, and Pieter collected instead Geertghe's valuables. Geertghe was imprisoned for five years, and died soon after being released.

Meanwhile Rembrandt and Hendrickje had a child, Cornelia, and lived happily together–unmarried–for 15 years. After Hendrickje died, Rembrandt lived alone with Cornelia. Titus married but died before his daughter, Titia, was born. Rembrandt lived to see his granddaughter, and died in the fall of 1669.

Light and Shadow

Rembrandt painted biblical scenes with unrivaled sensitivity and insight, with a genius that was arguably a divine gift, which might suggest that Rembrandt was a deeply spiritual man with a profound and authentic faith in God. The way he treated Geertghe, however, might suggest just the opposite. How could someone paint like Rembrandt did–and live like Rembrandt did? How could a transcendent artistic ability like his be joined with selfishness, corruption, and greed? Why was Rembrandt not made more noble and pure by the wonderful talent he was given?

These are very hard questions, because to answer them you need to think about what God is like, what human nature is like, how God treats people, and how people respond to God. They are also very important questions—good ones to talk over with your parents.

The Prodigal Son

Find Rembrandt's painting, "The Return of the Prodigal Son," and as you look at it, read the parable that inspired it (Luke 15:11-31). This is thought to be one of Rembrandt's last paintings, and one of his most touching. It is a solemn, tender picture of repentance and forgiveness, of "weary and sinful mankind taking refuge in the shelter of God's mercy."[5] Perhaps Rembrandt meant this painting to be a testimony of his own experience. Perhaps, at the very end of his life, this prodigal son, whose works were so inspiring to others, came home to the Father.

---

[1] Schwartz, G. (1985). *Rembrandt: His life, his paintings* . New York: Penguin Books, p. 22.

[2] Ibid.

[3] Slive, S. (1977). *Dutch Painting 1600-1800*. New Haven, CT: Yale University Press, p. 65.

[4] The WebMuseum is available at a number of sites. You can search for them using "webmuseum" as your search word, or find links to them at *metalab.unc.edu/wm*. At whatever site you choose, click Famous Paintings on the WebMuseum home page, then Artist Index to get an alphabetical list of artists, then Rembrandt to go to the Rembrandt collection.

[5] Slive, *Dutch Painting*, p. 96.

Read Chapter XVI

☐ Why do the Spanish decide to retreat from the siege of Alkmaar? (Give at least two reasons.)

☐ Describe the sea battle with the Spanish. How is the Spanish admiral, Bossu, captured?

☐ What bad news does Ned hear about the Countess Von Harp and her daughter?

☐ What is Ned's plan to free his friends?

Think It Over

How has Ned changed since the last time Peters saw him (see pages 258-259/276)? Has he changed in appearance only? Which of Ned's experiences do you think changed him the most? Have you had any experiences in your life that have changed you? What were these experiences, and how did they affect you?

Vocabulary

The following words are found in Chapter XVI. The definitions are provided for you. Write one paragraph (or if you really like a challenge, one sentence) that uses all five words correctly and still makes sense.

desisted – discontinued; ceased	page 256/273
intimidate – frighten; coerce	page 256/273
inundation – flood	page 256/274
acclamation – loud vote of approval	page 258/275
missive – letter	page 266/284

Activities

- Find out more about siege warfare.

- Ned leaves **Alkmaar** and returns to **Enkhuizen**. There he joins his father on the *Good Venture*, and with the Dutch fleet, attacks the Spanish fleet between **Amsterdam** and **Horn (Hoorn)**. After the battle he rejoins the prince in Delft. Then, hearing that the countess and her daughter were imprisoned in Maastricht, "He went first to **Rotterdam**, and bearing west crossed the river **Lek**, and then struck the **Waal** at **Gorichen**, and there hired a boat and proceeded up the river to **Nymegen (Nijmegen)**. He then walked across to **Grave**, and again taking boat proceeded up the **Maas**, past **Venlo (Venloo)** and **Roermond (Roermonde)** to **Maastricht**" (see page 265/284). Trace Ned's journeys on the map on page 66 of this guide. (Note: not all of these places are labeled on the map.)

Read Chapter XVII

- [ ] Describe how Ned rescues the countess and her daughter.

- [ ] Who is Requesens?

- [ ] What happens to the Spanish fleet that was sent to rescue Middleburg from the Dutch?

- [ ] What happens to Count Louis and the army he brings in from Germany?

- [ ] What do the Spanish soldiers do after defeating Louis?

- [ ] What happens when the Spanish soldiers receive their back pay?

- [ ] What do the people of Leyden do when the Spanish siege is temporarily lifted?

Think It Over

What cruelty does Alva commit at the very end of his reign? How does Alva treat those to whom he owed money? About what does he boast as he leaves the Netherlands? What kind of person does Alva show himself to be by these actions?

Vocabulary

All of the following words are taken from Chapter XVII. Get out a dictionary and look them up as quickly as you can. Read the definition of each word carefully and try to remember it, but don't write it down. Time yourself to see how quickly you can find each one. After you have looked up all of them, recall the definition of each word and write it down.

abominable	page 269/288
impudent	page 273/292
opulent	page 273/293
remission	page 273/293
apathetic	page 280/299

Activities

- **Write and Save**–What price does the prince pay for his devotion to his country (see page 277/297)? What does it show about his character that even after losing all this, he does not give up? Is he a lunatic or a hero to continue his seemingly hopeless fight against Spain?

- After rescuing the countess and her daughter in **Maastricht**, Ned journeys through **Bois-le-Duc** and **Rotterdam** to **Delft**. Afterwards, Ned takes part in a sea battle off **Walcheren Island**, during which the city of **Middleburg (Middelburg)** falls to the prince's forces. Find these places on the map on page 66 of this guide.

Read Chapter XVIII

☐ Why do most of the Dutch ignore the King of Spain's "pardon"?

☐ Why is it so difficult for the prince to convince the authorities to open the dykes?

☐ What things cause delays in the prince's plan to rescue the people of Leyden?

☐ What is happening to the people of Leyden during this time?

☐ What happens during the night just before the Dutch fleet reaches Leyden?

☐ What happens to Ned and where does he go?

☐ What surprise does Ned find when he gets home?

Think It Over

The Dutch were willing to ruin their own homes and farms by cutting through the dykes rather than surrender. In fact, "they were fully resolved die rather than to yield to the Spaniards" (page 286/306). What do you think about this? What do you think about the two men who accept the King of Spain's "pardon," renounce the Protestant faith, and return to the Catholic Church (see page 282/302)? Who does the best thing? Why?

Vocabulary

Read these (rather silly) sentences:

I was sent to reconnoiter the area along the beach, but we really thought the spy had slipped into the estuary west of the dunes. At any rate, he had disappeared, just as if he had dropped into oblivion. I couldn't help but think how demonstrative his thanks would be when he found out that we were prepared to offer him amnesty.

Now rewrite the sentences so that the overall meaning is preserved, **without** using the vocabulary words from Chapter XVIII listed below.

amnesty	page 281/301
reconnoiter	page 285/306
oblivion	page 289/310
estuary	page 292/313
demonstrative	page 295/316

Activities

- **Write and Save**–What do you learn about the prince's character on page 291/312?

- If you have a kitchen scale, weigh out 1/2 pound of bread and 1/2 pound of meat. This was a daily ration of food for an adult male–women and children got less.

- See the map of the city of **Leyden** on page 67 of this guide. Notice the defences around the perimeter of the city—the wall and the encircling river—and the gates (poorts).

Read Chapter XIX

☐ What is the "double game" the Queen of England is playing with the Netherlands?

☐ How does Ned's father feel about him going into the Queen's service, and why?

☐ Describe the conditions in the Netherlands during the two years that Ned carries letters back and forth. What is happening there? What is the Act of Union of 1575?

☐ The state of affairs in Antwerp is confusing when Ned arrives. Reread this part of the chapter (see pages 307-309/329-332) very carefully–perhaps more than once–and describe the situation on your own words.

☐ Who does Ned save (again)?

Think It Over

What do you learn about the character of Queen Elizabeth in this chapter? What sort of a person is she?

"The Prince of Orange was firmly resolved that all men should have liberty of conscience" (page 305/328). If you had been a Protestant in his day, would you have agreed? If you had been a Catholic? Why or why not?

Vocabulary

All of the following words are taken from Chapter XIX. Get out a dictionary and look them up as quickly as you can. Read the definition of each word carefully and try to remember it, but don't write it down. Time yourself to see how quickly you can find each one. After you have looked up all of them, recall the definition of each word and write it down.

trepidation   page 297/319
conclave   page 301/324
aspirations   page 303/325
concessions   page 304/327
peremptory   page 305/328

Activities

- If you were the prince, how would you try to persuade Queen Elizabeth to help you fight against the Spanish? Just for fun, compose a message designed to persuade someone in your family to do something he wouldn't ordinarily want to do—like cleaning your room for you, or doing some other unpleasant chore. What makes a persuasive argument effective?

- In 1575 the Spanish recovered control of the **Island of Schouwen**. Find this place on the map on page 66 of this guide.

Read Chapter XX

☐ What happens when the Spanish attack Antwerp? Why does the defense fall to the townspeople themselves?

☐ How do other nations react to the sack of Antwerp? Why?

☐ Philip almost makes peace with the Netherlands–what is the one point he refuses to agree to?

☐ The political events summarized in pages 323-326/346-349 and pages 330-331/353-354 are confusing. Reread this part of the chapter very carefully–perhaps more than once–and describe these events in your own words.

☐ Two very significant things occur in Ned's life in this chapter. What are they?

Think It Over

This is a confusing chapter, partly because Germans are fighting for both sides. The German soldiers are mercenaries, or hired soldiers, and fight for whoever pays them. As the Spanish and their Germans enter Antwerp, the Walloons (mercenaries from what is now Belgium who are fighting on the Dutch side) turn and run. Then the Germans fighting on the Dutch side actually desert to the other side and help the Spanish. Compare the behavior of these hired soldiers with that of the Dutch people (see the **Think It Over** question in Chapter XVIII). What accounts for the difference?

Vocabulary

Find the following words in Chapter XX, and using the context as your cue, match each word to its definition.

pandemonium   page 317/340
lissome   page 320/343
wanton   page 322/345
raze   page 324/347
parsimonious   page 328/350

demolish; flatten
lithe; supple
cruel; spiteful
chaos
frugal; stingy

Activities

- Just for fun, imagine that you must escape suddenly from your town, as the countess and her daughter must do. Where would you go? How would you get away without being seen or caught? What would you take with you?

Read Chapter XXI

☐ What happens on July 10, 1584?

☐ How do the Estates of Holland respond to this event?

☐ What is the importance of the river to the people of Antwerp?

☐ Describe how Parma closed the river.

☐ Describe the battle for the dykes.

☐ What is the situation in the Netherlands at the end of the book?

Think It Over

This chapter is a litany of mistakes that hurt the Dutch cause (there are more than a dozen mentioned). What are some of them? What causes these mistakes?

Vocabulary

All of the following words are taken from Chapter XXI. Find each word and, using the context as your cue, write down what you think it means. Now look up the words in the dictionary to see if you are right, and if not, correct your definition.

assassination	page 332/355
instigation	page 332/355
capitulation	page 333/356
negotiation	page 350/375
emancipation	page 350/375

Activities

- Using the map on page 69 of this study guide, trace the military maneuvers described in this chapter (from page 335/359 on).

Vocabulary Words from Chapters V to IX

abominable	capitulation	estuary	missive	peremptory
acclamation	concessions	impudent	negotiation	raze
amnesty	conclave	instigation	oblivion	reconnoiter
apathetic	demonstrative	intimidate	opulent	remission
aspirations	desisted	inundation	pandemonium	trepidation
assassination	emancipation	lissome	parsimonious	wanton

Review

Use the words listed above to complete the crossword puzzle on the next page. The clues are given below. Check your answers on page 71 of this guide.

	Across		Down
1	lithe, supple	2	nothingness
3	loud vote of approval	3	indifferent
4	chaos	5	expressive, effusive
6	discontinued, ceased	10	frugal, stingy
7	frighten, coerce	12	hopes, ambitions
8	discussion designed to reach	14	anxiety
	an agreement	15	abatement, lessening
9	arrogant, audacious	16	compromises
11	provocation, initiation	18	wealthy
13	unequivocal, absolute	19	survey for information
17	appalling	21	private meeting
20	surrender	24	immunity, pardon
22	flood	25	where a river meets the sea
23	cruel, spiteful	26	letter
27	demolish, flatten		
28	act of killing someone		
29	freedom, deliverance		

Prepare a paper on the Prince of Orange. Using the information found in an encyclopedia, make a timeline of the most important events in the prince's life. (If you can't find what you need under "Prince of Orange," look under "William I of the Netherlands" or "William the Silent.") Find a picture of the prince and use it to draw an illustration for your paper. Now gather together your answers to the **Write and Save** questions from Chapters VI, VII, XVII, and XVIII. Using these and information from the encyclopedia as your building blocks, write a paper describing the life and character of the Prince of Orange. In the last paragraph of your paper, tell what you have learned from studying the prince that can help you develop your own character.

Abject
abjure
abominable
abstained
acclamation
agitation
allusion
amnesty
apathetic
ascended
aspirations
assassination
assent
aver

Baffle
beleaguered
bigot

Canon
capitulation
cessation
clemency
compunction
concessions
conclave
confiscation
cordial
corroborate
countenance

Demeanor
demonstrative
deputation
deride
desecration
desisted
dexterously

diffident
discreetly
disdain
distraught
doggedly

Effigy
elevate
eluded
emancipation
embark
estuary

Facsimile
fervor
flurry

Heretic

Imbued
imperative
implored
impudent
inadvertently
incredulous
indefatigable
indignation
induce
inferred
instigation
intimidate
inundation

Lissome
listlessly

Malicious
meddle
mercenaries
metamorphosis
minions
missive
monotonous

Negotiation

Oblivion
omen
opulent

Pandemonium
parley
parsimonious
peremptory
pestilent
phlegmatic
placidly
pompous
portly
presumptuous
procure
prostrate

Raze
reconnoiter
remission
rendezvous
repulsed
reticence
rites

Stupefied
subdued
sublime
subsidy
succor
sumptuous

Tedious
trepidation

Voluble

Wanton

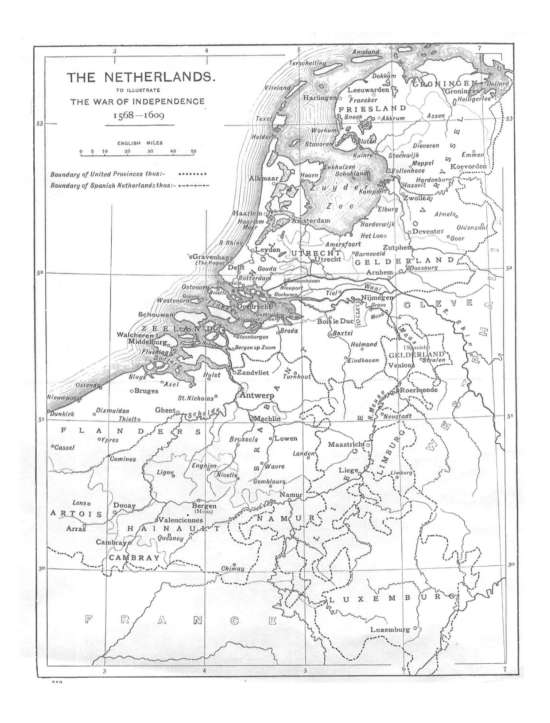

PLAN OF THE TOWN OF LEYDEN

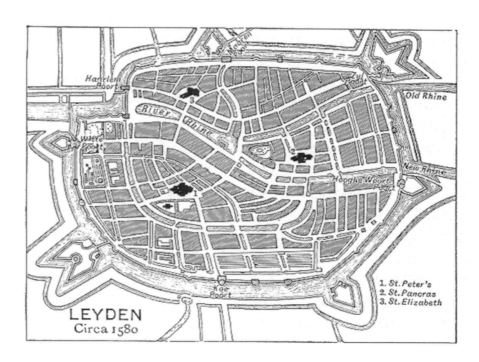

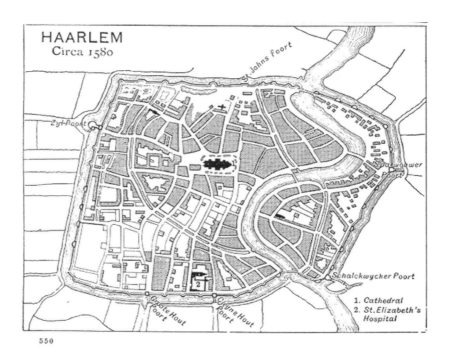

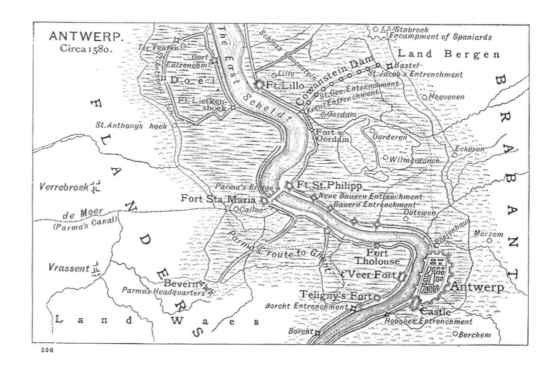

Vocabulary Review 1

The incorrect sentences are numbers 1, 2, 4, 5, 8, 12, 15, 16, 17, and 20.

Vocabulary Review 2

	M	E	T	A	M	O	R	P	H	O	S	I	S			R			
	E			B						U		U				E	M	B	A	R	K
	D			J						B		B				T			
	D	E	M	E	A	N	O	R			D	I	S	D	A	I	N	
	L			C						U		I				C			
	E			T		A	B	J	U	R	E		D			E		
			P			B				D		Y				N		M
			P			S										C		A
		C	O	U	N	T	E	N	A	N	C	E			E		L
			S			A											I
A	G	I	T	A	T	I	O	N			R					C
			R			N				I		A	L	L	U	S	I	O	N
	I	N	A	D	V	E	R	T	E	N	T	L	Y			O
			T			D				E				V		U
	O	M	E	N			P	R	E	S	U	M	P	T	I	O	U	S
		I					A							L
		N			C	O	R	R	O	B	O	R	A	T	E		U
		I					L							B
		O					E							L
		N					Y		D	I	S	C	R	E	E	T	L	Y
		S												

Vocabulary Review 3

The incorrect sentences are numbers 1, 2, 3, 5, 7, 10, 11, 12, 14, and 20.

Vocabulary Review 4

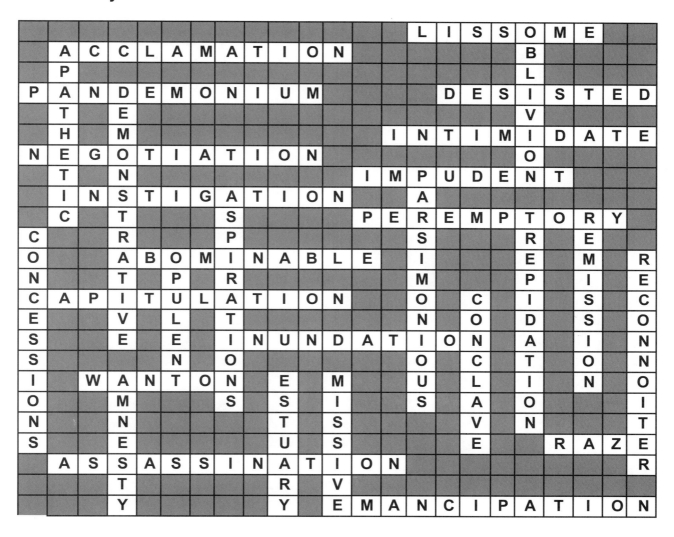